BAILEY
THE BIG BULLY

BAILEY
THE BIG BULLY

By Lizi Boyd

Viking Kestrel

For Danny, Jonathan, and Gwen

VIKING KESTREL
Published by the Penguin Group
Viking Penguin, a division of Penguin Books USA Inc.,
40 West 23rd Street, New York, New York 10010, U.S.A.
Penguin Books Ltd, 27 Wrights Lane, London W8 5TZ, England
Penguin Books Australia Ltd, Ringwood, Victoria, Australia
Penguin Books Canada Ltd, 2801 John Street, Markham, Ontario, Canada L3R 1B4
Penguin Books (N.Z.) Ltd, 182–190 Wairau Road, Auckland 10, New Zealand

Penguin Books Ltd, Registered Offices: Harmondsworth, Middlesex, England

First published in 1989 by Viking Penguin, a division of Penguin Books USA Inc.
Published simultaneously in Canada
10 9 8 7 6 5 4 3 2 1
Copyright © Lizi Boyd, 1989
All rights reserved
ISBN 0-670-82719-3

Set in Plantin Light

Bailey was a big bully.

Every day on his bike he'd find a big puddle
and spray you with mud!

He shoved and pushed. He HAD to be first in line.

And you HAD to give him anything he wanted.

He HAD to eat your cookies at lunch!

He told big stories. And you HAD to listen.

He made up all the rules. And you HAD to play HIS WAY!

If someone dared say, "But Bailey, that isn't how you play," he'd glare and hiss, "Quiet, SISSY, it's MY game!"

And if the ball went out into the high,
wet grass, he'd shout, "Go and get it!"
And you HAD to go.

And if you didn't go he'd pull your hair
and whisper, "Don't you dare tell!"

Everyone was scared of Bailey. He was big
and bad and mean.

And if you did tell the grown-ups always
said the same thing, "Ignore him."

Everyone did what he said because
no one wanted Bailey to pick on them.

Then a new boy, Max, came to school.

He didn't know who the bully was and he
didn't care. When Bailey pushed Sam down,
Max helped him up.

When Bailey was playing marbles HIS WAY,
Max said, "I know another way to play."
Bailey snarled, "It's MY GAME!"

But Max just walked away.

And at lunch, Bailey said, "Give me your cookies!" But Max said, "I'm going to eat mine!"

Even when Bailey kicked Max and
whispered, "DO what I SAY!"
Max said, "Hey leave me alone."

One day Bailey was telling his big stories
and Max asked "Who wants to come to my
house and build a tree fort?"

Everyone went to Max's. They looked at all the trees and picked a good one for the fort.

The next day Max heard Bailey say to Sam,
"Don't go build that stupid fort!" Stay
HERE I want to play ball!" Then he took
Sam's arm and twisted it until he screamed.

Max didn't think. He bopped Bailey right
in the nose. Max got into trouble.

The grown-ups said, "Apologize." Max said,
"I'm sorry about your nose but why do you
have to be such a bully?"

Bailey didn't have a clue about having friends.

Now everyone was ignoring him and playing
with Max.

One day Max said, "Hey why don't you come and see our fort?"

Bailey growled, "Leave me alone."

But he hid in the high grass and watched.

Max saw Bailey's gray jacket and yelled down,

"Come on up and look around."

Bailey climbed slowly up the ladder.

When he got to the top he said,

"Okay, now I'll tell everyone the rules."

But Max said, "Hey this is OUR fort.

We make the rules TOGETHER.

You can't be a bully here!"

The fort was cool. Bailey wanted to help.

So he brought boards from his house.

Max was happy that he was helping.

When it was finished Max said, "I have a surprise.
Everyone cover your eyes."

Max nailed a small sign at the bottom of the tree.

"Okay," he said. "Now you can look."

In red letters it said, "BULLIES KEEP OUT."

Everyone cheered! Even Bailey.

And then Max put his arm around Bailey and said,
"Isn't it more fun to be a friend."